All children have a great ambition to read to themselves... and a sense of achievement when they can do so.

The **read it yourself** *series has been devised to satisfy their ambition. Since many children learn from the Ladybird Key Words Reading Scheme, these stories have been based to a large extent on the Key Words List, and the tales chosen are those with which children are likely to be familiar.*

The series can of course be used as supplementary reading for any reading scheme.

The Sleeping Beauty *is intended for children reading up to Book 2c of the Ladybird Reading Scheme. The following words are additional to the vocabulary used at that level —*

king, queen, palace, trees, not, happy, baby, magic, will, princess, good, fairy, see, bad, she, cut, her, finger, spindle, die, sleep, long, time, cannot, asleep, everyone, sleeping, beauty, princes, down, prince, kisses, awake

British Library Cataloguing in Publication Data
Ainsworth, Alison
    Sleeping Beauty.—(Read it yourself. Fiction.
    Reading level 2; 8)—([Ladybird books]. Series 777)
    1. Readers—1950-
    I. Title   II. McBride, Angus   III. Series   IV. Series
    428.6   PE1119
    ISBN 0-7214-0855-9

First edition

Sleeping Beauty

retold by Alison Ainsworth
illustrated by Angus McBride

Ladybird Books Loughborough

Here are the king and queen.

This is the palace.

It is home for the king and queen.

Here are the trees.

Here is the water.

The king and queen
are not happy.

They want a baby.

A fish is in the water.

It is a magic fish.

The fish says,
You will have a baby.

The king and queen
are happy.

They have a
baby princess.

The king says to the good fairy, Come and see the baby princess.

The bad fairy
wants to come.

The king says, No!

The good fairy comes to the palace.

She has magic toys
for the baby.

She is happy
to see the baby.

Here is the bad fairy.

She has no toys
for the baby.

The princess will cut
her finger on a spindle
and die, she says.

No, no! say the
king and queen.

The good fairy says,
She will not die.

She will cut her finger
on a spindle
and go to sleep
for a long, long time.

The king says,
We cannot have a
spindle in the palace.
The spindle has to go.

21

Here is the princess.

This is her dog.
They have fun.

The princess has a ball.

The dog can jump
for the ball.

The king and queen
are not in the palace.

The bad fairy comes.
Here is a toy for you,
she says to the
princess.

It is a spindle.

The princess
has cut her finger
on the spindle.

She is asleep.

Her dog is asleep.

The king and queen come home.

They see the princess, asleep.

They go to sleep.

This is the palace.
Everyone is asleep.

Here are the trees.

Here is the water.

The princess is asleep
for a long, long time.

She is the
sleeping beauty,
says the good fairy.

Some princes come to the palace.

They want to see
the sleeping beauty.

They cannot cut down
the trees.

This prince wants to
see the sleeping beauty.

He can cut down
the trees.

He sees the palace.
Everyone is asleep.

In the palace,
he can see the king
and queen, asleep.

He can see the dog,
asleep.

He can see the princess.

This is the sleeping beauty, he says.

He kisses her.

Look! The princess
is awake and she can
see the prince.

Come, says the prince.

They go to see
the king and queen.

The king and queen
are awake.

The king kisses
the princess.

The queen kisses
the princess.

The dog is awake.

He is happy to see
the princess.

Everyone in the palace
is awake.

The good fairy says,
Bad fairy,
you have to go.

We do not want
you here.

The king says,
Go home, bad fairy.

The prince and princess
are happy.

The king and queen
are happy.

The dog is happy.